Rechenka's Eggs

Written and illustrated by

Patricia Polacco

Philomel Books NEW YORK

To Vladimir Pozner and Phil Donahue
for "bridges" of understanding

Copyright © 1988 by Patricia Polacco.
All rights reserved.
Published by Philomel Books,
a division of The Putnam & Grosset Group,
200 Madison Avenue, New York, NY 10016.
Published simultaneously in Canada.
Printed in Hong Kong by South China Printing Co. (1988) Ltd.
Book design by Nanette Stevenson

Library of Congress Cataloging-in-Publication Data
Polacco, Patricia. Rechenka's eggs. p. cm.
Summary: An injured goose rescued by Babushka,
having broken the painted eggs intended for the Easter Festival
in Moscva, lays thirteen marvelously colored eggs to replace them,
then leaves behind one final miracle in egg form
before returning to her own kind.
ISBN 0-399-21501-8
[1. Geese—Fiction. 2. Easter eggs—Fiction. 3. Eggs—Fiction.
4. Soviet Union—Fiction.] I. Title.
PZ7.P75186Re1988 [E]—dc19 87-16588-CIP AC

Seventh Impression

Babushka lived alone in a *dacha*, a little house in the country, but she was known far and wide for the fine eggs that she lovingly painted. Her eggs were so beautiful that she always won first prize at the Easter Festival in Moskva.

Each day Babushka would take the shell of an egg from her basket and paint it in wonderful designs, using the shapes of stars and flowers, triangles and circles. Through the long, cold winter Babushka painted.

Then one day after a snowstorm, Babushka went outside. She could still hear the faint sound of falling snow. It was a sound like soft rain. Herds of caribou came to feed at Babushka's because the grasses they usually ate were covered with snow.

"A miracle," she whispered as she fed some. "These wild things have found their way to me."

Just then a flock of noisy geese honked loudly overhead. As they glided over the snow, one of them faltered and fell from the sky. Babushka went to where the goose lay crumpled in the snow.

"A hunter did this," Babushka grumbled.

She carefully picked up the goose and took it back to her little house.

There she fed the little goose from her own table and put the goose in her best basket lined with the warmest quilt from her own bed.

"I shall name you a good name . . . one that we both can like, eh, my little friend?" she said as she patted the goose's head. "How do you like Rechenka? . . . Yes? Then Rechenka it shall be . . ."

With Babushka's care, Rechenka grew stronger as each day passed. To repay her kindness, Rechenka laid an egg for breakfast every morning.

As Rechenka got better, she waddled around the little house exploring every nook, cupboard and corner. One day she jumped on top of Babushka's worktable, overturning the jars of bright colored paint that she used to color the eggs.

"Niet!" Babushka screamed as she chased the goose with a broom. "No!" The frightened goose flapped her wings to get away and knocked over the basket of eggs that Babushka had so lovingly painted. The eggs crashed onto the floor and shattered into millions of pieces. They were both very sad. There was no reason now for Babushka to go to the Festival.

The next morning Babushka slowly got out of bed and trundled over to Rechenka's basket to get her morning egg. But when she reached into the middle of the quilt, she picked out the most brilliantly colored egg that she had ever seen. "A miracle," Babushka whispered, "a miracle!"

She made small holes at both ends of the egg and blew the yolk and white into a dish to cook and eat later for breakfast. Then she held the egg up to the morning light and marveled at its beauty.

After that, every morning for twelve mornings there was another egg, each more beautiful than the one laid the day before. Soon Babushka had enough eggs to take to the Festival in Moskva.

How wonderful, she thought. A miracle has replaced the eggs that were broken.

"Spring is here my little friend," Babushka said to Rechenka the morning of the Festival. "Soon now you will be flying off to the north with your flock."

She bustled to the hearth fire and brewed some of her most favored tea. The two shared a saucer of tea with *kulich*, a sweet Easter bread. She covered each piece with *pashka*, a spread of cheese, butter and raisins. They savored each bit together.

"One for you . . . one for me," Babushka chanted. "Da . . . da . . . my little friend, I shall sorely miss you, but you are a wild thing . . . and a miracle sent you to me. It would not be right to ask you to stay here with me forever."

When Babushka left her little house, she took one last look at Rechenka sitting on the doorstep. She waved, then took determined steps for Moskva with the basket of her precious eggs.

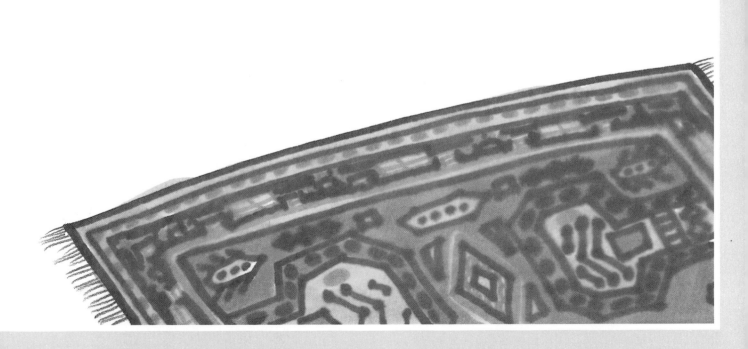

She crossed Lebitov Valley where the caribou mothers were walking their newborn calves. A miracle, she thought. New little lives . . . a miracle. She crossed the bridge over the Moskva River and soon she could see the onion domes of Old Moskva.

The Festival was bright and exciting. There were goat carts selling *kulich* . . . processions . . . dancers . . . jugglers and laughing children playing and running. Babushka showed her old friends the eggs.

Her eggs are the most beautiful in all Russia, they thought.

"Look at them," the elders said. "They almost glow . . . as if the paint is part of the shell itself."

The judges picked Babushka's eggs as the most beautiful! Babushka was so happy. She beamed as she looked at the First Prize . . . a feather-bed quilt!

As Babushka made her way homeward, a honking flock of geese flew overhead. Babushka gave them a long lingering look. She wondered if Rechenka was one of them.

When Babushka arrived at her home that evening, Rechenka was gone. Alone, she put the new quilt on her little bed. She brewed a cup of tea, ate the last of the *kulich* and *pashka*, got into bed with her favorite book of poems and drifted off to sleep.

She hadn't noticed Rechenka's basket.

But that night Babushka was awakened from a sound sleep by an ever so small sound. It was coming from Rechenka's basket. She hobbled closer and saw a glorious egg! But this one was different from all the others.

It quivered and moved.

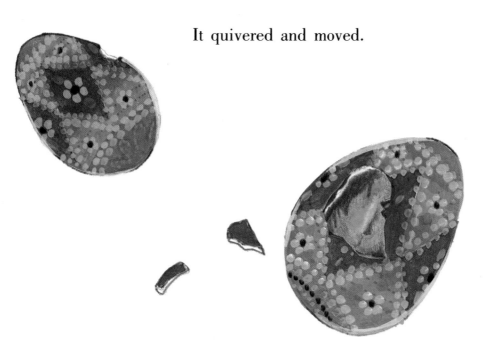

It made tiny muffled sounds.

The egg jumped, bumped, rolled and pitched in the basket.

Then, there was a crack and Babushka could see the very special gift that Rechenka had left for her. "All a miracle," Babushka said.

And this little goose remained with Babushka always.

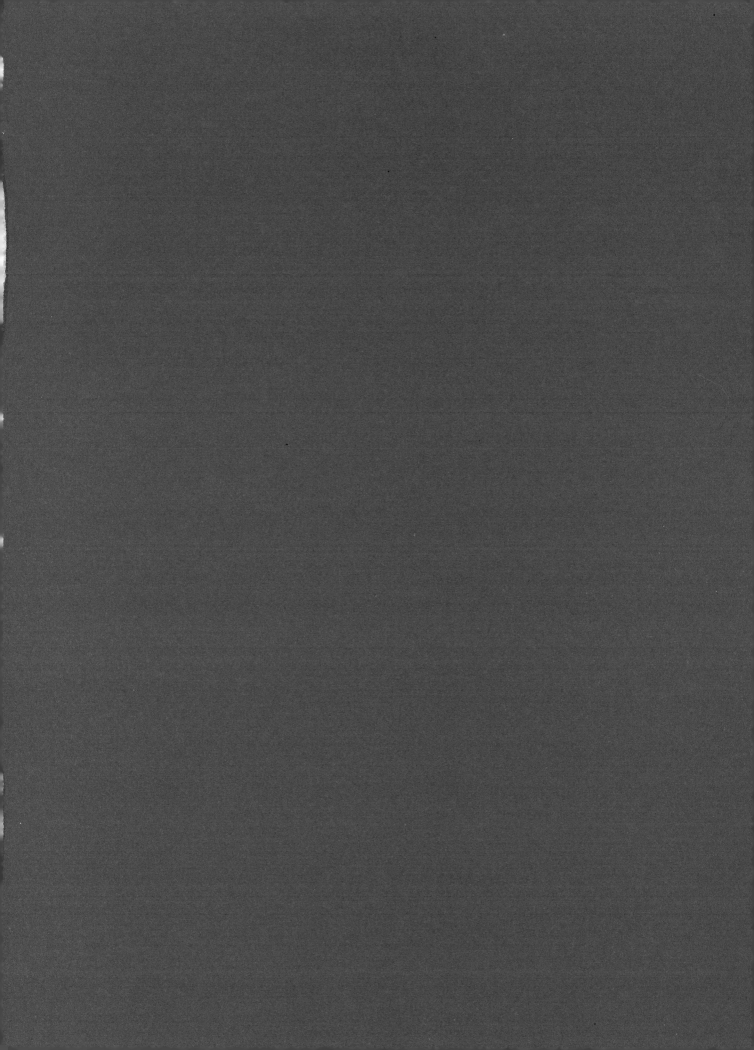